# Love, Lost Below The Lunar Lampposts

Table Of Contents

2

Canto 1

of

Love, Lost Below The Lunar Lampposts

My tommy gun's larynx is jammed,
while aiming at our cabin on the beach.
No echoes blast across the sand.

And there's our cabin's slanted stance.
Like a ghost, inside asleeps the old me.
His tommy gun's larynx will be jammed.

Behind my back the sea revamps
as waves retune their slurred and shushing speech.
No echoes blast across the sand.

I halt upon the quiet land,
and pull the trigger, anxious for clattered screams,
but my tommy gun's larynx is jammed.

The tiny clicking clicks again.
Fifty bullets stay inside the drum magazine.
No echoes blast across the sand.

This tommy gun becomes the most unloyal machine.
 The trigger- pulling, pulling, pulling sorry-clicks for me.
My tommy gun's larynx is jammed.
No echoes blast across the sand.

I pull the trigger. All I hear are *clicks* again. Agitated *clicks*.
*Click. Click. Click.*

I wanna watch the windows shatter,
hear the tommy gun's clattered laughter,
hear my  happy-ever-after spatter,
hear its wooden teeth begin to chatter like it never mattered.
I wanna spray a haze of racing strains of bullets
and hear the splinters crack and scatter.
*Click. Click. Click. Click. Click.*

I wanna watch the cabin tatter-
collapse against the flash of blasting bullets
before I get even more madder.
*Clickclickclickclickclick.*

I wanna watch the logs and windows stagger,
hear this bladder full of bullets blabber
as I feel the madness getting fatter.

Aphrodite was writing novels bout us,
one which Cupid never meddled in
as she analyzed our haunting tones of humming
which cauterized the hour before our sleep.
Aphrodite held her pen above us,
contemplating why-so our romance baffled her.
Aphrodite had scratched her noggin, perplexed.
Bewilderment. Writer's block. A thousand second thoughts.
Abandonment never threatened coupled-us.
Aphrodite failed. Her pen and powers shrivelled
because she never caught the awe between us.

Our laughter croaked as lanterns shone
inside the bars the size of barns.
As February kissed the coast,
she fell asleep inside my arms.

Repeating nights, the lampposts smirked
when she pulled me in and out the bookstores
before returning to our home
where we would own the wilting winter chill.

We owned the wilting winter chill.

The month of March, the snow was slush
as melting snow witnessed our trust build and build.
Beside the fireplace's hums
we napped and owned the wilting winter chill.

We owned the wilting winter chill.

As mornings rose, I'd hold her close,
and dressed with ruffled sheets we slept.
Migrationary yawning croaked,
as seagulls returned to their nests .

Our peaceful cot, her body soft,
asleep upon the mattress made by us.
The lucky pillows matched our hair,
 but the tommy gun's all I cradle now.

The tommy's all I cradle now.

Good morning stance, request a dance,
with my arms extended welcoming and proud.
With waking smirks, we took our hands,
 but the tommy gun's all I cradle now.

The tommy's all I cradle now.

We laughed and ran on speckled sand.
Night revealed its diamond ashes.
Aquatically clapping hands
eavesdropped inside the Atlantic.

As Gloucester slept, we'd meet in bed
and whisper plans about the boulevard.
We held congress about the day
inside our lonely cabin on the beach.

Inside our cabin on the beach.

With tired tones, we'd plan our meals,
and add modern prophecies to recipes
before we woke to morning's teal
inside our lonely cabin on the beach.

Inside our cabin on the beach.

With oven-mitts, she'd leash my waist,
and murmur stories on my neck.
Reactionary chuckles came
as my hair was combed by her breath.

Her humming voice, its poised guidance;
she hushed against my collar while I stirred.
We meshed together in the hug
like by-stranders in the business of light.

Stranded in the business of light.

Against the stove, she held me close,
and I stayed silent to hear her warm advice
as our soup began to bubble
for by-stranders in the business of light.

Stranded in the business of light.

She'd pick our clothes for April strolls,
and let me wear my white T-shirt.
Involuntary smiles rose.
She asked me what looked good on her.

I picked it out, it's Christmas cough,
it's faintest green carolled around her form
inside the bedroom's sunny scene.
I watched, betrayed by the pear colored blouse.

Betrayed by the pear colored blouse.

Her soil hair, it matched the pear.
I worshipped the blooming smiles on her mouth,
pleased with what we chose to wear.
I loved, betrayed by the pear colored blouse.

Betrayed by the pear colored blouse.

In the evenings, we'd both relax.
She sat up-right upon the sand
affectionately combing back
my yellow hair with gentle hands.

My blond was nestled on her blouse
like a fallen lemon under pine trees,
asleep below the pricking pine
as I had laid my head inside her lap.

I laid my head inside her lap.

We held Depression's funeral.
Her brunette spirals bounced whenever she laughed.
I lived the safest miracle
when I had laid my head inside her lap.

I laid my head inside her lap.

Upon the docks, we'd sit and talk.
The sea watched us like a mirror.
Ocean-libraries dipped and bobbed,
but I read nothing of water.

Below the teal, as daylight peeled,
we'd point and watch the boats escape the bay.
A foreign twinkle woke in her eyes.
I watched, betrayed by the pear colored blouse.

Betrayed by the pear colored blouse.

Regretful leash, the kisses' speech
that began appearing down her sudden frowns
after pecks above our coffee.
I loved, betrayed by the pear colored blouse.

Betrayed by the pear colored blouse.

Sunny mornings, in the kitchen
we would go through mail together
with ordinary handwriting
skiing down the bills and letters.

Ink and sharpies, black as coffee,
laying like retired crowns on paper,
watched our tired smiles mimic
the two cursive names upon our mailbox.

Cursive names upon our mailbox.

The pencils scratched our names abreast.
A kiss above the table's vanilla cloth;
we stamped our envelopes of breath
like the cursive names upon our mailbox.

Cursive names upon our mailbox.

A wilting hug, its loosened grip.
"My Love, is everything okay?"
Debilitating oven-mitts
contemplated against my waist.

In our cabin, its wooden tomb,
arguments became portraits around me
as all reassurance crusted.
Drying guilt was glowing in the darkness.

Guilt was glowing in the darkness.

As daylight paled, and kitchens frailed,
her "I love yous" sounded like a final breath
in the dullest pear colored blouse
as her guilt was glowing in the darkness.

Guilt was glowing in the darkness.

We walked the shore, alone and warm
before the light began to cool.
Love's affinity joined our arms
as laughter blessed the tidal pools.

Exploring hands, collecting shells
that we'd string across our bedroom ceiling
when candles wept their melting wax
as sleeping stars appeared above the beach.

As stars appeared above the beach.

Sleepy balance, farewell laughing,
died inside my white shirt and her blouse's seams
as birds departed on the wind
before the stars appeared above the beach.

As stars appeared above the beach.

She'd read my palm, and hold my arm
as cups of tea relaxed and cooled.
Exploratory fingers marched,
predicting what tomorrow brewed.

With final sips, our tea vanished
and left behind its muddy mulch of dirt.
Her eyes descended down my cup,
and moped, "I'm gonna leave you, Nicholas."

"I'm gonna leave you, Nicholas."

Her diving eyes, they read the leaves,
and foretold my future with regretful breath.
Disciplinary warnings creaked.
She warned, "I'm gonna leave you, Nicholas."

"I'm gonna leave you, Nicholas."

Drinking coffee at the table,
she whimpered like a piano
like the cheats in confessionals
when she told me she had to go.

Distraught and shocked, I listened hard
as truth about her identity slipped.
All the things I thought were stories?
She told me she was a mermaid.

She told me she was a mermaid.

Our eight month romance died away
as every reason came for her not being able to stay.
So bluntly that confession.
She told me she was a mermaid.

She told me she was a mermaid.

I watch my shadow hold the tommy
the way a widow holds her bouquet.

It's a slim and skinny silhouette,
dowsed upon the sand like spilling ink.

All a written pen has done has died,
and tides erase our haunting footprints.

The widow's shadow and I have nothing else to say.
We read each other's minds.

The tommy flings its jamming out bullet.
The widow's shadow casts away her ring.

My tommy gun becomes a furious typewriter,
sharply shrilling out forty-nine farewells forever.

Without regret, my tommy types our break-up letter,
sharply shrilling out forty-nine farewells forever.

With hissing breath, it hurries ink from out the silencer,
sharply shrilling out forty-nine farewells forever.

And cursive's dotted all across the cabin's timber,
sharply shrilling out forty-nine farewells forever.

The angry journalist's revolting in my fingers,
sharply shrilling out forty-nine farewells forever.

Forever, forever, bullets leave this typewriter.
Forever, forever.
Sharply shrilling out forty-nine farewells forever.

Shards of shattered glass begin to cry
as my tommy continues to whine.
Brighter than diamond rings, the golden casings
put Aphrodite in retirement.

In a cloud of dust, the splinters fly.
The logs begin to crack and untwine.
Bullets sing, swimming in, as my spraying swing
puts Aphrodite in retirement.

Bullets rupturing the cabin's hide-
specks of wood disperse below the sky.
Destruction, hissening, sending bullets in
as Aphrodite starts retirement.

Fire.
Broken, orange.
It gropes the cloudless blue
as empty tommy clings to me,
tired.

Fire.
Puffy, blackened.
Sunlight pulls its wool
probably from a bursting pipe,
tired.

Fire.
Cracking, roasting.
Black colognes around me
in a field of bullet casings,
tired.

Cologned with fire's wool, I twist around,
silent and sullen like my tommy gun
as ashy flakes are rolling down my back
throughout my disembarking steps away.
My steps begin parading down the sand,
across the grains of white where Love explored
as ash is snowing on the plain of white,
but I limp away, refusing to frown.
The cracking, hissing, charring, whispering,
begs my stay inside the wilting cabin,
but I limp across the sand with tommy.
He's empty, but reminds me that it's done.

The casings glimmer like forty-nine wedding rings.
Their gold cylinders slump around me in the fluffy ivory
sand,
so shy and timid that they'll all remain orphaned and
abandoned.
Lucky me, the empty tommy gun's my brown and black
bouquet
as casings glimmer like forty-nine wedding rings,
and that ablazing cabin's roaring like an organ- forever
burning.

Canto 2
of
Love, Lost Below The Lunar Lampposts

Icing.
Aging, stiffing.
Rigid wooden buildings,
foaming up below the sunlight,
whitened.

Icing.
Laying, hearing.
Sand pretends its sugar,
bowing under boulevard's stare,
young again.

Icing.
Baking, freshened.
The cake of buildings sleep,
but remain awake forever
for people.

Ivory buildings wake,
like a row of macarons
stacked along a sheet.

Their edges' are baked through,
but the sun adores to bake,
so they're always fresh.

Dollops of shingles
mimic oak colored icing
with a rustic touch.

Half the boulevard is missing.

The strip of pavement
humbles any fancy dish,
still the pastries chirp.

The buildings settle,
waiting in the seaside sun,
distracted with tides.

Half the boulevard is missing.

The runt is burning.
The weird macaron's aflame,
lonely on the beach.

Half the boulevard is missing.

And all the water,
swishing tidal lullabies.
Waves refuse to help.

Half the boulevard is missing.
There's a beautiful piece missing.
It'll not be baked again.

Warm's that romance between the sea and cafes.
A crabby chill is crossing sidewalks,
late for dates with steam against the window panes.
They collide outside bakery shops.
The brine's attracted fast by clamshell colors
that the strip of buildings proudly flaunt.
This Love, the ocean couldn't want another,
sheltered like the wine inside restaurants.
Frowning gusts of wind become the bowing guests
throughout this salt-polluted wedding
in the mornings, in the night and its darkness,
where vacation is never pending.
Like Romeo and Juliet without the feud,
the seafaring romance is never doomed.

I'm sitting on that unloved end of the boulevard
as every window looks past me;
a seemingly nameless man on a jetblack bench
with a tiny satchel tucked between his sneakers.

Very few folks have said hello to me
upon their daily passings since I've sat down here.
I enjoy it though, feeling like a ghost
while I watch the elegant stretch of buildings ignore me.
I keep my focus on the windows as police motorcars pass by
me,
presumably a ride for local detectives or investigators.

The grey and speckled mess of the sidewalk is admiring me,
but I'd rather seek a flirtatious gaze that escapes the
windows all down the boulevard.
Their regal excellence doesn't want me,
and it makes me want their attention more.

The curtains without any wrinkles behind smudgeless
windows.
The harmony of white and wooden walls below indigo
roofs.
The sleeping lampposts with nothing to say.
I want to be a part of all of it, and I feel I am a baby in the
tummy
 while adoring storybook sea-faring worlds asleep against the
atlantic.

And it's an interesting day in this fairytale about a sea-faring
town,
because someone just burned their cabin down.

It's sadly beautiful inhaling that harmony
that the sea and boulevard have created.
It's got the whimsical salt of the sea,
and the smoky curse of mankind-
chasing one another in a wicked long necked bottle,
sideways on the earth.

"I heard the fellow's name was Nicholas,"
rumors the crowd upon the boulevard
as police search the beach for arsonists,
wandering round the burnt remnants of logs.
As different breeds of folks observe the beach,
they'll never know it was me.
A breed of police motorcars gallop,
all crossing dune and dune of empty sand,
and stopping at the cabin's grey carcass;
a black and charred and brittle skeleton.
As different breeds of cops observe the beach,
they'll slowly know it was me.
"Did the couple living in there survive?"
"It was such a quaint appearing cabin
The rumors fly with disagreeing whines.
"Dear, beauty isn't fire repellent."
The different breeds of folks observe the beach.
They'll never know it was me.

A flock of students appear across the street,
all resurrected out from classroom graves
like hallucinations conjured by coffee
as they laugh; no longer locked away.
Amongst their solar flare of laughter,
I swallow coffee, black and steaming
like I'm watering a tree with hot tartar;
just a local in the cafe, daydreaming.
Siting in the booth against the window,
I watch a police sergeant waddle in,
greeting waitresses without a sorrow
as they ask him what he is ordering.

In the ashes on the sand,
amongst the bullet casings,
silhouettes remain.

They must have out their notebooks,
walking round the cabin's guts,
rude with little pens.

Studying my shadowprint.
I'm a little proud of him,
but the dread remains.

Rude with little pens,
picking up the clues;
they'll search for me soon.

That library looks more like a courthouse;
an experiment from the ancient Greeks.
It's sable marble steps and pillars yawn,
turning beige below Massachusetts' tans.
I am an eager archaeologist,
and a deserting soldier in a jam,
while awing at the  pillars on the stairs
as such a warm library blushes beige.
Maybe I'll find a lesson while hiding
If footprints disappear below the dust,
I'll get a chance to read about a tale,
escaping what parade of stress I've charmed.

Novel.
Unlocked, open,
bathing in the lamplight
under the librarian's lips,
thinking.

Novels.
Padlocked, abhorred,
drowning in the bookshelves.
They're wishing to be read by her
glasses.

Novel.
The second page.
My entrance interrupts.
She looks upon my face's page,
reading.

As if ascending to an outer space full of sunsetting clouds of
gas,
we climb a flight of stairs towards the second floor,
and enter into that tomb of bookshelves where the light is
greater.
It wafts around me like a ghost.
Humbled by the broken hallway of bookshelves,
I feel as if I should bow before them,
but the way in which my librarian guide struts forward tells
me there's no use.
I just follow her down the ranks of bookshelves,
smelling how the sunlight enters through the windows to
singe away the dust.
A warm charcoal aroma blasts itself across our way
as every book begins to melt alike a candle.

There must asleep a book about mermaids.
Napping where? I fear in every corner.
Threatening covers that portray mermaids-
this library's labyrinth's minotaur.
I feel a fast repulsing pulse throughout me.
Mermaids model on the novels' covers.
Why cast my heart again against the sea
like a toddler fishing under thunder?
The widest bliss deserves entrustment,
but I vanished in a lie for months,
and found myself a lost fellow abandoned
to cradle that affable tommy gun.
What I'd cradle in a second heartbreak
 if I kissed a librarian,
and she too became a secret mermaid?
I shouldn't let myself explode again.

Afraid about the gills upon the necks I'll kiss,
 I stumble down the boulevard again.
Perhaps I should forever just retire my lips
before another woman swims away again.
But, oh, what a lovely librarian?
She harbored hope against her glasses' bay.
Oh, but my ex was a lovely woman-
whose barb-wire throat withheld the truth.
Ah, I'm a lonely man upon a sad account as such.
I'll never kiss again, and that'll do.
Let it do everyday.

The tide is crashing on the sand upon my right,
and interrupts my mind's iambic rambling.
 I'm returning down the diner's lullabies
as waiters spin around their **OPEN** signs
as my heart remains padlocked for librarians-
afraid to hear another mermaid sing.
I'm closed. Nobody is allowed in.

I'm mourning who I used to be
when I pass gardens that are black and white.
Only the roses' stem stay green
with their petals white and sorry.
I can't tell what color they used to be.

Like a jazz musician who forgot how to play,
I ramble far away, only for another song to taunt me-
another black and white garden sleeps against ivory
mansions.
Those snowy pillars stand so proud above the lack of color.
They were never yellow, pink or orange.
They're blandly excellent in white.

Another patch of flowers weed and wave
behind a strip of picket fence- pointy like shark teeth.
Grunts of green try spying on me as I pass.
They beg for help behind the fence,
holding onto green between the gaps.
But black and white everything pulls me away
only for another garden to green-greet me the same.

In the inn and in its hallway,
I'll find myself confused tomorrow
while waking up below the velvet curtain
as sunlight wilts its purple sorrow
when I wake beside awful revelations.
I spread a scarlet blanket on the floor.
What a sight for eavesdropping sunlight;
a lonely man asleep upon the floor.
I wish I saw the lies behind her eyes.
Now I fear mermaids instead of cops.
They'll catch me like a king inside a cave,
awaking on my homemade scarlet cot,
but they'll never catch this distrusting pain.
When I finish smoothing out the covers,
my heart decides I'll not be like my former lover.
If I'm caught- I'll tell the truth- if I'm caught.
I'll tell them everything,
then all of Gloucester will hunt mermaids until extinction.

The razor's scratch is jazz against my chin.
It's such a sad and sorry symphony
as summer passes that romantic bliss
til it's music in the cemetery.
But that mermaid never liked our song I suppose.
I wonder what she listens to now-
digging bout the shipwrecks, searching for gramophones
as sharks remain upon the prowl.
Like a scythe against the yellow wheat,
I swiften that exploring blade across my chin
then let it scrape the foam off of my cheeks
before I shave away the whitest past again.
 It all erupted into orange flames.
It should stay that way.

Her mourning stance, requests a dance
with arms extended limp and proud.
Imaginary second chance
that she asks to wear like a crown.

This wishful dream, the hallway melts
her ghost appears alike a screaming bride
as velvet curtains turn to black.
I try to swat her cobweb palm away.

I swat her cobweb palm away.

Without a doubt, confessing mouths,
they whisper what I wanted to hear her say.
Her ragged gown, a paling silk.
I try to swat her cobweb palm away.

I swat her cobweb palm away.

It's 4 a.m, and I'm awake,
sitting on the familiar docks.
Listening to the water talk,
asking where she went.

The town of Gloucester stays asleep
as Aphrodite's clock is ticking;
calls from literary agents,
asking where she went.

My bowing head awaits nothing.
Splinter shredded pillars hold me up
as I mope and slouch upon the edge,
asking where she went.

Is that a real mermaid below me?
Circling in alluring paces
like a curvy serpent in the sea.

Dark enough is this weird mystery
as water begs with voices frantic.
It's not a real mermaid below me.

Hope ignores the water's warning speech
as that anomaly swims and paces
like a curvy serpent in the sea.

What a whimsical pace the blob keeps,
cycling below the blue surface
as if a real mermaid's below me.

Just a blob is beautiful to me
as that affable hope is faceless
like a curvy serpent in the sea.

I edge against the dock's wooden edges,
and slip between the sea and air, I'm falling
to that real mermaid beside me
like a lie I always believed.

Water swallows me.
I'm caught inside its fingers,
cold and freezing hold.

Puffing out my cheeks,
awaiting razor kisses.
The shark approaches.

Indigo candles,
they wither underwater,
and try to warn me.

Rough the shade of grey,
such a vanilla belly.
The shark proposes.

Where's the violins?
Its jaws propel and open
before I say "yes".

That indigo net refreshes up and down my spine.
I slip and slump below the silky blankets
like a little drowning ant inside blueberry wine-
a quick entrance inside a foreign planet.

I squeal and flail my arms around below the surface.
The shark approaches like a conscious missile
with eyes so dilated, hungry, black, they're depthless.
She's my eager bride racing down the aisle.

Ocean ambience,
in untuned silence,
a great white wedding,
paranoid and frozen.
There's no mermaids.

Piano teeth applaud and clap apart the water.
The bubbles fizz and pop as we thrash about.
I yelp. The shark's a clutz and not a gentle lover.
I hug its side and roll throughout the current.

Next to snapping jaws,
clinging on her side,
diving straight and down,
hearing teeth cut the sea.
There's no mermaids.

The shark leads me in a dance through a sideways spiral

as bubbles spin throughout our fits of twisting.
She keeps me on her sable gown of bulky muscle
with romantic constant attempts to bite me.

I punch its snout,
slowed by water,
furious fists.
Air running out.
Water's getting dark.
Continuous punching
above her mouth.
It snaps again,
closing, opening.
Punching, biting
like bashing cymbals.
Crashing, crashing.
I slip away.

As police wave, I limp away from help.
Bruised and bloody, I limp across the sand.
I felt a solace in the great white's mouth.

They wave and wave, requesting that I halt,
but I'm paranoid they know who I am,
so police shout. I run away from help.

They flee away from blackened cabin's stump,
breaking into sprints with friendly hands,
but knew no solace in the great white's mouth.

I wonder just how I managed to get out
while breaking into a sprint across the sand
as police chase. I run away from help.

Concerned, unaware, they run now as well,
chasing strange-me up the sandy land
after I escaped the great white shark's mouth.

Bruised and bloody, I run and flee the sand
on a beach where my tommy gun was jammed.
The police chase. I run away from help.
I felt a solace in the great white's mouth.

I bow my head throughout my morning walk
with blood appearing down along my face.
It's drying to the shade of apricots.

Does the sunrise know I survived the shark?
It's awfully orange like a peach today.
It cranes its head throughout my morning walk.

With tattered sleeves ragged and damp with blood,
the locals aim their passing awkward gaze.
Faces blush to the shade of apricots.

The rumors stir as they begin to talk
with such a fellow like me on his way,
bowing his head throughout his morning walk.

"This bloody man exploded his own house."
The whispers must foretell a police chase,
ending in a puddle of smashed apricots.

They'll never know as I limp away,
a man attacked by sharks and left by Love just needs a break.
I bow my head throughout my morning walk.
Blood's drying to the shade of apricots.

Thelonelymanislimping.
Thelonelymanislimping.
Thelonelymanislimping.

"Look away. Look away."
I hear the mothers say to their children.

Thelonelymanislimping.
Thelonelymanislimping.
Thelonelymanislimping.

As couples hold their hands,
it's embarrassing crying in public.

Thelonelymanislimping.
Thelonelymanislimping.
Thelonelymanislimping.

Disappointed patrons;
these folks pretend they don't notice my pain.

Thelonelymanislimping.
Thelonelymanislimping.
Thelonelymanislimping.

Their glances write this like they're students in detention,
writing such a phrase a thousand times on a chalkboard.

The whites of every eye is scratching the obvious across my
face.
It's such a dusty tattoo running down my face
as I limp and drag my crying self away from everyone.

Thelonelymanislimping.

Do they wonder where he's limping to?
I know he's limping through his apoclolypse
with a bobbing head and swaying arms,
he cries through every step, ignoring every glance
as he limps, and limps, and limps.

# Canto 3
## of
## Love, Lost Below The Lunar Lampposts

A doughy baby face is in the black and white.
I know his scruff of hair is blond
behind the black and white curtain against the wall
on the tanning bricks of the bar.
But I'm not feeling very wanted.

Illegal firearm possession and arson?
An eight-thousand dollar reward?
And well they used my high-school yearbook's photograph.
Their wanted man's in Gloucester,
but I'm not feeling very wanted.

The flower girl of law and order left this here
like a petal on the pavement
after a shark consumed the groom and swallowed him.
They want him, blame him, now chase him,
but he's not feeling very wanted.

Kicked out by the inn-keeper.
She saw my wanted poster.
She said me coming back all bloody was a red flag,
but I never got the chance to explain the shark attack.
She phoned the police
as I fraudulently promised to send a check
for my nap I took in the second-floor hallway,
and I stumbled out before the cops arrived.
Oh, what a headstart again.
Ratted out before I could explain
in a free-verse stammer
that wants to be let out like a name bleeding down a
mailbox.

I stand behind the boulevard's raven-railing,
and watch the priests, police and people pray
on the beach with candles melting grief away
because she's labelled missing, gone or dead.
But they'll never know, I want her back the most.

Her friends and locals join the candlelight vigil
with bowing heads above the ink of ash
where that affable kitchen once nurtured my Love.
But they'll never know, I want her back the most.

The boulevard behind me's drunk with wanted posters.
It's me on the paper that is staring.
He's the one who knows, I want her back the most.

Oh, could I shout "she's alive below the sea"
to clear my name? Tell them what she told me.
I'm the one who mourns the most tonight.
But they'll never know, I want her back the most.

I walk around with a lantern on the beach,
looking for mermaids, or a spot to dig my grave,
while police search for me.

I prowl about below the night's warning sheet.
Crossing sandy banks, tiptoeing along the way,
I walk around with a lantern on the beach.

Throughout the tidal coughs of apologies,
there's the lantern's haze against water's indigo shade
while police search for me.

I haven't caught a glimpse of eyes in the sea.
But there goes my gaze, scanning for her in the waves
as I look around with a lantern on the beach.

My wanted posters' stapled to the trees,
 search parties parade through taverns and alleyways
while police search for me.

Crossing sandy banks, tiptoeing along the way,
looking for mermaids, or a spot to dig my grave,
I walk around with a lantern on the beach
while police search for me.

Now the beach becomes a church without a ceiling.
This ivory emptiness is promising throughout my search for
truth;
on the prowl for some mermaid to throw in the
confessional booth.
I guess they're hiding underneath the secular net of sea
when the beach becomes a church without a ceiling.
Dunes of wedding-gown-colored sand pray silently with
faith never-ending.

Fishing.
Open, bare-hands.
I know I'll catch nothing
because the drooping waves promised.
Nothing.

Fishing.
Chilling, empty.
Blue against my ankles,
brown below the silky surface.
Nothing.

Fishing.
Like a surgeon
left a tool inside me.
The pliers sleep below my gut.
Poking.

The drunkest patrons
never notice anyone is missing,
They hold their vigils
at the very bottom of their bottles.

So a Gloucester tavern
swallows one of my moping feet whole
as the hunching drunks
watch me pass my wanted person poster,
and turn away to drink.

The police are gone,
busy on the beach or at their houses.
They hold their vigils
in the arms of their understanding wives.

So I order a beer,
seated next to scruffy looking bums,
and the bartender's
seen too many wanted person posters
to recognize my face.

Where's the music?
My ears recall the gramophone's arrows
when I held my vigil
in her arms throughout a mellow paced dance.

I'll share my story here

to the stinky bloke beside myself.
His crusty eyes yawn
as they pass my wanted person poster.
I've earned his respect.

Love the second beer
slipping down my throat alike candlewax.
It'll hold vigils
if I ever wake up tomorrow.

They're probably still there,
pretending that they all befriended her,
forgetting of me
til they pass my wanted person poster
to mold fake memories.

"The man she lived with?"
"Oh, what a strange one, who never talked much."
They hold their vigil,
whispering about me, knowing nothing.

The bar's silent and safe.
It's loud for folks with guilty consciences,
but mine is empty
when I see my wanted person poster;
the guy I thought she loved.

They hold their vigils.

I ignore my wanted person poster.
They hold their vigils.
I ignore my wanted person poster.

Romantic illness leaves the lampposts.
Love's lost below the lunar lampposts.

Sober stumbles down the pebbled road,
I limp again below the lunar lampposts.

In this town with night with blankets made of coal,
so dull the light from lunar lampposts.

Closed windows know I've nowhere to go.
I limp and wince below the lunar lampposts.

So pale a kiss against my lack of hope.
I'm only kissed by lunar lampposts.

Why this shade is wilting that romantic glow,
I'll never know,
because the Love is lost below the lunar lampposts.

The world is mute because she's not with me.
What the seaside sunlight said was for her.
Nothing's ever wanted to speak to me.

The lampposts pale, the sea's begun to sleep.
All their lullabies were only for her.
I think they're mute because she's not with me.

A sorry cough of light begins to wheeze
under lampposts where I once walked with her.
They have never wanted to speak to me.

Gone's the music raised by the symphonies
in the theatres where I once danced with her.
I think they're mute because she's not with me.

The puddles on the pebbled roads will freeze
where I once skipped through April rain with her.
They have never wanted to speak to me.

I wander down these places without her,
almost limping, falling, lost without her.
I think they're mute because she's not with me.
They have never wanted to speak with me.

I told my aunt about the girl I loved
on a bench in Florida during June.
I can only imagine how dumb I smiled,
as I discover how much I miss that conversation,
telling her everything about her,
about how proud I always was of the girl I loved.

And now I curl up on the sand
in another Massachusetts' August.
Oh, how the sand absorbs a tear so easily.
This vast curtain of wrinkled sand is not a bed. It's a sponge.

And as night becomes a hungrier adventure,
the people on the benches disappear,
and the tide is softening its lullaby
as I remember how I smiled
when I told my aunt all about the girl I loved.

August always haunts a fella like me.
There's not a door to knock upon the sea,
but its smack against the sand invites me.

Would seagulls deliver any letters?
I'm sure they'd drop it like they drop the crabs-
a book with spoiled endings' on the ground.

Like a lover's sent to luny houses;
I'm growing more afraid to visit one.
I'll meet the wrong patient with great-white rags.

The threat of summer ending stains this month,
and past situations make it a haunt.
August's the month of sick and dying Love.

I ponder on the sounds of being born.
A cinematic echo, a tuneless harp.
It plucks above the cellos
just before the violins decide to wake up.
I often wonder if that's the sound of adventure-
an uncatchable string of golden sound,
melting into the world.

What's the sound when you walk away?
When you stop looking.
I hope it's peaceful.
Then again, what have I heard?
Could I let myself believe another word from anyone?

I'm mad, and everything's silent.
What's the noise of peace?
Play for me. Play for me.

I beg my bagging eyes to let her go.

God. God. Let me choke
as rain verdunns the charcoal-colored road.
Like the tommy's speech,
the rain is shrill throughout its peddling.
Scratch my craning neck.

God. God. Take me home
to that April melody in the kitchen.
Re-stir the pot of time.
But an empty beach is catching rain now,
laying still like the dead.

God. God. Love is cold.
Shrivelled in the chilling silk of goosebumps.
My hair is matted down
as I limp alone throughout 3 a.m's watery chains,
spearing on my shoulders.

Lanterns perch atop the blackest pillars
as I'm skulking on and like a miser,
prowling past the posh accent of fences
to meet a ghost inside his apartment.
I beg my bagging eyes to let her go.
Just a mist allows itself to watch me,
stalking right behind me down the sidewalks
in a vein departing the boulevard.
I beg my bagging eyes to let her go.
Some thunder spills its ink across this street,
letting warnings crash against the windows
as I beg my bagging eyes to let her go.
What parades of healing take this long?
I beg my bagging eyes to let her go.

The indigo-gowned Fates are running out of ink.
Every step's a soliloquy as I trip throughout my stagger.
The woman in the pear colored blouse is my red floating
dagger,
leading such a character like me down the road through the
rain.
The indigo-gowned Fates are running out of ink,
so such a scene repeats across the stage, a madman follows
what he thinks.

I'm pining over never playing house again.

If I wasn't on the run, I'd probably attract realtors.

They'd show her and I through a neighborhood of friendly gardeners.

"What a lovely kitchen? Help me stir the soup with hugging arms."

I'm pining over never playing house again.

She's most probably living in a shipwreck's skeleton with some merman.

Alone, he hides amongst his former peers.
Well, they don't recognize him anyway.
And when passing lanterns hit their glasses
the flutes of champagne strobe across the ceiling,
and he knows just how to hold it
in the dolphin colored suit.
Pretending to talk with the socialites,
the young appear so uninvolved with me,
well, the me on the wanted poster's gloss.
Lonely men are handsome when they don't talk.
My tongue knows just how to rest.
What a dolphin colored suit.
Hiding in the Gloucester nightlife,
pretending to be like the others;
too young to be on wanted person posters.
I grieve the sheriff on the hunt for me,
for being well-dressed makes me feel together.
And they can't catch me in this buzz.

Hiding in the asteroid belt of parties.
College kids ignore tomorrow
in the mansions, in the villas
in an upside-down France-like town
where lust'll linger in the night.

Hiding in the asteroid belt of parties.
Turning down potential angels,
afraid about the gills they hide.
I hold my champagne like a cross.
I think I'll leave early tonight.

Hiding in the asteroid belt of parties.
Walking past interested lips
with disinterest dried below mine.
I look around for escape routes
even though the cops are outside.

When did Love become apocalyptic?
Planetary rings are ripped apart by kisses.
My Saturn-looking heart is wilting,
sending fragments all across a cosmic canvas.

How my Love disrupted my calm orbit.
Extraordinary is the bulb that is spinning
behind my chest below my suit,
sending fragments all across a cosmic canvas.

Beautifully, my Saturn spun before,
but it's rolling out of the solar system now,
and rolling into lightless voids,
sending fragments all across a cosmic canvas.

I feel I've left a safer world as she's below the sea.
She'll never see my planet's rings disintegrate,
sending shattered fragments all across a cosmic canvas.

\

I'm barging into cathedrals.
I do it sane and sober,
sliding over ivory tables.
"She's a mermaid! Don't trust her!"

Crashing in through wedding venues
with police right on my tail.
Parade about and warn the grooms.
"Add water, she'll grow her tail!"

The bridal party's furious.
Champagne bottles miss my head.
Stalked by police sirens' chorus.
Gee, I'm finally wanted.

Perhaps, stained-glass was made to break.
"Check her neck for gills and scales!"
Their weapons blare as I escape
another wedding off the rails.

Running, vases crash and scatter
through scarlet venue lobbies,
away from Love that never mattered.
I'm enjoying my new hobby.

Well, the automobiles chase me.
I sneak inside the churches
"Have you tried putting her in the sea?"

and leave with brand new bruises.

As altars become abandoned,
the groomsmen try and catch me.
Loose because I'm on the run,
and she's below the sea.

I'm crashing weddings
on these yellow shaded days,
afraid for others.

Warnings in my eyes,
the folks recognize my face
from wanted posters.

Before the cops come,
I warn the groom in a haste
before the "I do".

Oh, I shout and croon
"your bride could be a mermaid",
like mine, oh, like mine.

A groggy grey is napping on the roofs
as ridges on a vanilla macaron
allow their crumbled style upon the walls
of barbershops, restaurants and banks and bars.
The slanting shingles all await a nun
throughout their nap upon an orphanage,
together like a field of dead ravens,
unaware upon the whitest villas.
I feel them shrink and shrivel, grey and dull.
They're sweating under that annoying sun.
It'll beat me grey until I'm a shingle
like the napping ones above me on the run.
The sun is dripping down those praying roofs
as down the boulevard I move and move.

Return my falling mind to quiet dreams
of slow and swaying spins upon the sand,
before black-holes appear above the beach.

A campfire dims and dies by dancing feet
where final fits of laughter dare to land,
returning falling minds to quiet dreams.

Indigo sheets remain above the sea
as perhaps one more smile may understand,
before black-holes appear above the beach.

Allow a palm to stop my chance to sleep,
and steer my face to recognize my plans
about my falling mind and quiet dreams.

As sand becomes a shade of sable grief,
the horizon becomes awkward and bland
before black-holes appear above the beach.

As prayers become conjured by lonely hands,
requesting some angel to rescue Man,
release my falling mind to quiet dreams
as my black-hole appears above the beach.

Let me wake along tomorrow's river
when the rowing oars of pain have vanished
as flakes of auburn promise me better
with ends for such a broken heart's famine.

I'm hiding in an apple orchard
below the indigo apologies that the night presents,
but the clouds forget their "sorry" is meant for me.

I'm all alone between the rows of trees,
afraid to pluck an apple.
They're pretty, red and gleaming in the lampless night.
All I have is that reflection on their skin.
Their pretty, pretty, pretty warnings shine.
They must be poisonous.

The farmer's oldest daughter wakes me up.
Propping up against a tree, I squint through sunlight.
Her wicker basket's empty, but she's happy.
Her tilting head and bobbed hair greets me,
but I run away. I run away.
She must be poisonous.

All alone, I visit Venus's tomb;
trying not to look for you.

And fitted in my dolphin-colored suit,
I'm holding back, "how could you?"

It's like I'm making a cup of tea with a fork.
The tea, and every other thing, begins to slip between the
cracks.
I wish I had my kitchen wall to smash and throw my teacup
at.
I want nothing to do with misfit silverware from here on.
It's like I'm making a cup of tea with a fork,
and I just don't have any caffeine to keep my rage asleep
anymore.

Aphrodite writes with brisk and nimble fingers.
I can't constantly read this book about mermaids and love
again.
The book's a long mystery, but it's my only reading option.
If she truly still loves me, then why did she abandon me?
Aphrodite writes with brisk and nimble fingers,
but I'm flipping past the pages, past this end- I still am
craving answers.

My freezing hand,
my freezing fingers
shiver all alone
below the lunar lampposts'
pale and wilting glow.

My haunting breath,
my cloudy breathing
slithers all alone
below the lunar lampposts'
pale and wilting glow.

My freezing hand,
my freezing fingers
will be held again
inside a solar angel's
frail and loving hold.

Love will not be lost below the lunar lampposts.
These plutonian pillars slick themselves with freezing ghosts
of rain,
and drip around me like the tears which I know deserve to
be sang,
but a candle still revives the light throughout the coldest
storm.
Love will not be lost below the lunar lampposts.
My destined angel will light and light and light and light the
sickest candle.

Canto 4

of

Love, Lost Below The Lunar Lampposts

The train begins its iambic chugging
like a heartbeat across the railroad track
underneath the night's purple-veined biceps.
And, now I know, I'm never going back.
Pass the line of trees, retired farmlands,
I watch the window flicker like a screen.
That alluring film is dull and plotless.
True stories makes me want to fall asleep.
The train ignores the land it races past,
but the lakes and ponds are waving calmly.
The night is breathing on the blades of grass,
but I hear nothing about such a scene.
The blues of night are dancing on the Earth
like a silent film accepting color.

They're advertising mermaids at the carnival.
She could be brushing back her hair inside these gold and
scarlet tents,
safe before her vanity, unaware about my wandering
as I pace and pout around the popcorn-vendors and
psychics.
They're advertising mermaids at the carnival,
but I only pace around with denial as cotton-candy spirals.

I find my wanted poster in the freakshow,
between the bearded lady and siamese twins
on the wall where circus advertisements flow.

Like an advertised rejected-Romeo
there hangs my lame, colorless, expression.
I like my wanted poster in the freakshow.

It hangs there like I'm part of the carnival
alongside the poorly paid attractions
on the wall where circus advertisements flow.

It's hanging, looking like it's found its home
as obscure signs surround me with acceptance.
I like my wanted poster in the freakshow.

Upon the wall, no longer all alone
with clowns, werewolves, and ancient-dressing men
on the wall where circus advertisements flow.

Without an inn, without a cabin,
I crane my neck with proud astonishment.
I love my wanted poster in the freakshow
on the wall where circus advertisements flow.

I walk about the anchored scarlet wagons
with children laughing at seesaws of fake affection,
and watch how the ringleader treats the lion
in a bonfire of hopeless hallucinations.

The carny's cracking whip.
The lion's whining growl,
chained with rusty steel,
poking in his neck,
while the children laugh.
I feel like him.

I shun away and bow my noggin downhill.
Ambient carnival pianos croak and stammer,
and grease the smoky night with xylophone shrills-
continuous four notes, played by a clown that's hammered.

His wobbling head.
Perma-lipstick smile.
His bouncing ankles
tapping on the bottles
while the parents laugh.
They'll fire him.

My curious noggin swivels back and forth-
my trusty compass leads me down the tents and circus.
Delirious bobsleds full of prizes
watch me pass as kids are throwing plates at bowling pins.

The crashing clangs.
A toddler crying.
He wants to go home.
Prizes layer shelves.
They're falsely promised.
I'm cracking.

I enter like a groom engaged to disappointment.
The gypsy-psychic wears a purple turban.
The wagon's red wallpaper wraps around us loosely,
pretending that it already knows the future.

The psychic takes my hand,
over oval wood,
with her pondering blinks.
Her face already knows
my first question.
"Does she still love me?"

Faint, her nail's a steamboat, crossing what my knuckles
hide.
Mute, anxious, I watch her thumb explore the curves.
What a chiselled hand, I've clenched it shut for all this time.
Leaning close, I watch the psychic's lips unpurse.

Shocked with parted lips,
under waiting eyes
with that awaiting blink.
The psychic's hands retreat
from what she saw.
And I ask again.
"Does she still love me?"

Our hesitation plummets like a crashing statue.
Her mouth opens, and all suspense is wilting.

"She loves and misses you, young man, and thinks about
you."
I'm washed with joy upon my fortune's telling.

With bliss ascending,
glances sharing joy,
sympathetic happiness.
Her power's syringed
romantic revelation.
"She still loves you."

The twists and turns mimic a carousel.
Between the tents, my feet parade, desperate for answers,
but I'll bow and make myself presentable,
and politely stop myself from blurting out curse-words.

In the nipping dark
carnival ambience,
floating on the dirt.
Lanterns bleed, they're sick.
Looking for their nurse,
I'm stranded.

I stomp the dirt and skid across a left turn
as freezing stratospheres apply their starry lip-gloss.
I'm late for wine with a beautiful stranger,
probably fresh out of the water, she's drying off.

Before a red tent
amongst the wagons' tombs,
stopping on the dirt
with a studious glance,
reading arrow signs,
I'm stranded.

The tent is lacking in a door for me to knock on.
I stumble in through velvet flaps with golden tassels.
A rubber-tail awaits me on the floor.
A woman, that I've never met, turns around. She's startled.

Sharing shock between us.
My answer on the floor,
her twinkling tail,
shooting down my dreams-
hopeful hot-air balloons,
crashing in the circus.
Was I lied to?

Tailpiece.
Lifeless, scaly,
it twinkles in the dim,
lying hollow like a paper.
Plastic.

Tailpiece.
Lime and neon,
it's flat against her toes
like a flattened garbage barrel.
Plastic.

Tailpiece.
Sparkles glimmer
across the pine of scales.
All imagination swims away.
Plastic.

The actress locks me in her catching hold.
Her hands forgive the shake throughout my arms
as palms descend and rise with gentle pace,
looking for survivors on my bicep.
We kneel together on her costume prop
below her vanity's warm atmosphere
with that ignoring mirror like a grave
throughout her hushing words, my trembled weeps.
She thwarts away my weak apologies,
explaining that she hates the tail as well,
which draws a chuckle out my frowning mouth
before she tells me everything's alright.
Before I talk about previous days
where Lost became my new last name.

I become a popcorn vendor,
Dressed in a barbershop quartet disguise,
telling carnies that my name is Tommy.

Flirtatious winks from the mermaid.
She's taught me my trans-atlantic accent.
I use it when I wish the kids farewell.

They love the new popcorn vendor
because relief's asleep behind his eyes,
waking up whenever someone says "hi".

Flirtatious joy from the mermaid.
We work across from one another
throughout the carnival's visit in the town.

What secrets haunt popcorn vendors?
Only that mermaid across the way knows,
but my yesterday is safe with her.

Working as a popcorn vendor,
I feel suddenly safe from *her*.

The boy upon the wanted poster disappears.
The actress cuts my hair with care before her mirror in her
tent
around the cough of eleven o'clock through our
conversations.
As Nicholas becomes an unsuspecting popcorn vendor,
the boy upon the wanted poster disappears.
I'm blending in, relieved, realizing that mermaids were never
real before.

Shooting glass bottles,
the tiger-keepers shoot first
with tents behind us.

Bored, I fold my arms,
recognizing the echoes
the planet swallows.

Reloading, it's my turn.
Revolvers never comply,
stubborn in my hands.

The bottle on the fence is right before my eyes.
Green and empty, sitting like an eager hooker in the brothel.
I got my aim. I pull the trigger, but no bullet's jetting out.
And all I feel is that revolver trying not to giggle
as bottles on the fence are right before my eyes.
This rabbit-sized revolver's jammed and quiet even after all
this time.

She says she'll run away with me.
I watch her glossless lips excavate my only wish.
"Being a mermaid is boring anyway.
This life isn't temporary."

She lulls my nervousness to sleep,
caressing such a boyish face I kept frozen yesterday.
Laughing bout the day we met inside her tent.
"This life isn't temporary."

After hours, meeting secretly.
The color pink becomes its very own emotion
in the scarlet haze of these carnival days
where life isn't temporary.

Well, it's karaoke night in the carnival.
As we listen to the songs we wished would last a little
longer,
we're all dancing like abandoned angels drowning in the
thunder.
My smile wears relief as that police asteroid is passing.
And it's karaoke night in the carnival.
Just a normal popcorn vendor, lost amongst the crowd, free,
uncatchable.

The circus takes its midnight nap.
The tents appear to shiver
as wagons hum with lanterns.
I'm taking such a chilling bath.

Icy in my wooden barrel,
underneath the violet rivers
pierced with dots of platinum stars.
The theatre-tent is watching too.

I crane my neck to love the stars.
Am I their admirer?
Only when I'm not hunted.
No longer hunted on the beach.

Her plastic tails are hanging on a rack
like the skins of slaughtered krakens.
She's wearing something far from being green
as lanterns radiate against our stance.
My wanted poster's on her vanity.
Its disorganized stare is watching us.
It's black and white amongst the lantern breath.
There's warmth against the dancing obelisks.
Perhaps, I found a woman worth my trust.
I feel the lantern's whispered answer, *yes*.
This feeling's bleeding down the silky walls;
I found the place my broken heart belongs.
My wanted poster's on her vanity,
and Aphrodite pleads insanity.

Just when I find a solar system in her eyes,
the police arrive.

They drag me out, across the ground,
betrayed by the pear colored blouse.
The lawn becomes identical colors
just when I found a solar system in her eyes.

And all the carnies can't believe their eyes.
The police arrived.

The earth's as parched as rotting pears,
betrayed by the pear colored blouse
as twenty coppers drag me far away
as all the carnies can't believe their eyes.

Just when I find a solar system in her eyes,
the police arrive, the police arrive.
All the carnies can't believe their eyes.
The police arrived. The police arrived.

Canto 5

of

Love, Lost Below The Lunar Lampposts

We owned the wilting winter chill.
The tommy's all I cradle now.
Inside our cabin on the beach,
stranded in the business of night,
betrayed by the pear colored blouse,
I laid my head inside her lap,
betrayed by the pear colored blouse.
Cursive names upon our mailbox,
guilt was glowing in the darkness
as stars appeared above the beach.
"I'm gonna leave you, Nicholas."
She told me she was a mermaid.
Betrayed by the pear colored blouse.
Betrayed by the pear colored blouse.

Sweating in my cell,
my back is slumped against the wall,
slouched below the thoughts
of her in the pear colored blouse.

Her friends wrote me,
and say she's in Finland now.
She's needed money
since I burnt our cabin down.

She's living freely,
selling what's left of herself.
I hope she's happy,
hooking in her pear colored blouse.

Prison walls are wedding gowns with stains;
broken promises, broken plans.

Guards are leaning on the popcorn bricks;
boring ornaments, boring men.

Lawyers in the cafeteria.
Cursive signatures, cursive names.

The warden waddles round the tables,
taking evidence, shaking hands.

I'm in a summer camp of shackles.
Snapping pickaxes snap the earth.

I'm sitting in my cell
like I'm on a plane about to crash.
The only passenger who isn't screaming.
I spiralled long ago.

My fingers on my chin,
thinking, slouching on the stale mattress.
The only prisoner who isn't sleeping
at three in the morning.

What about the angels?
An orange pair of hands'll catch me
the way I thought she caught me
in the carnival.

It's like I'm learning how to cry again,
choking on the chains she left around me.
The angels string their needles out and in—
making sure this hurt will never leave me.

Angels will whimper at my film's premiere.
They'll blow their noses in their cloudy seats
throughout my movie in Heaven's theater.
They watch me shoot the tommy on the beach.

The ghost throughout the strip of land between the cells is
tan.
It's what the sunlight used to be.

The guards will hush a reaching hand
when it's slipping out the bars to touch the dusty linger
of light which asks where goodmen went.
That luggage below my eyes knows the answer.
*I'm in here.*

No fingers ask for help here.
They curl against my chest to pray,
and pray as light becomes a graveyard of sand throughout
the hallway,
which we walk three times a day.
Breakfast, lunch and dinner.

Love was never lost,
right here, in my soul's strong and reaching glow.

Lampposts can't compare.
Their blurs are just a pale portrait of Love.

Love was never lost.
My soul is warmer. That's why light is cold.

Lamps and lanterns blush
when I let my heart shine beyond enough.

Below the water, in the carnival,
in the library, on the boulevard,
below the ceiling in my prison cell,
in the jaws of sharks,
and all around my noose tomorrow-

Love was never lost.
It follows me wherever I go.

The priest's calm understanding hand comforts me in my
cell.
He sits upon my mattress as I yank on his raven robes.

He pats my shoulder as if I'm some abandoned puppy,
and I explode with sobs against these black curtains draped
down the bed.

"Well, father, seeing that you're here,
could you do me one favor and exorcise her out of me?"

He gives a pleased and sorry look as he shakes his head no.
And as I beg upon my knees, he asks about my final words.

"I've tried absolutely everything else a man can try.
Slap a crucifix on my chest, and exorcise her out of me."

I draw myself across the cave-wall in my prison-cell.
A faceless figure twists around with Tommy napping in his
arms.

With brushing thumbs, the wall becomes a primitive canvas
with the burning cabin in the background like a wooly
mammoth.

That moment from history, plucked from fingers that
caused it,
is my proudest tattoo on the ivory-bricks of purgatory.

I love the lonely man amongst nothing except the sand,
standing in the lake of heartbreak, filmed again on the
prison-wall.

Let the lawyers, let the wardens, let everyone,
let a million eyes become a visitor inside my cell.
See how I freed myself.

When I'm hauled across a hill by police,
crowds of locals gather at the gallows-
all afraid about becoming like me.

They dressed me in a shirt with tattered seams
and stubble that I grew inside the jail,
now I'm hauled across a hill by police.

They've come to watch my final tragedy.
They circle all around the wrinkled oak-
all afraid about becoming like me.

A skinny noose awaits me at the scene.
A masked executioner tied its rope
when I walked across the hill with police.

I know they've all been waiting patiently,
with pouts of anticipation aglow-
all afraid about becoming like me.

What a way to go. What a way to go.
And, well, I hope they all enjoy the show.
When I'm stopped below the noose by police,
all are scared about becoming like me.

Without remorse, her eyes emerge
deep inside the pond of people.
Discretionary guilt is perched
on her face, afraid and feeble.

Her silent eyes mimic a deer
as twisted knots caress my bowing head.
I wonder where her voice has gone.
I wait, betrayed by the pear colored blouse.

Betrayed by the pear colored blouse.

A final time, our eyes collide,
but I think she'd never even blame herself.
I look with millions of "why's",
and wait, betrayed by the pear colored blouse.

Betrayed by the pear colored blouse.

The pear colored blouse becomes my omen of death.
There she is in the crowd, the woman who made Love
become a fear.
Her deering eyes apologize about nothing throughout her
stare.
This arsonist's about to hang, but why won't she clear my
name?
The pear colored blouse bec

www.ingramcontent.com/pod-product-compliance
Lightning Source LLC
Chambersburg PA
CBHW020731160726
47993CB00006B/2414